W9-CNX-131

Ten Little Puppies
Diez perritos

ALMA FLOR ADA · F. ISABEL CAMPOY

Ten Little Puppies

adapted from a traditional nursery rhyme in Spanish

Diez perritos

adaptación de una canción infantil tradicional

English version by Rosalma Zubizarreta · Illustrated by Ulises Wensell

rayo

An Imprint of HarperCollins Publishers

Acknowledgment and Source Note

To Rosemary Brosnan and María Gómez,
guardians of tenderness in the hearts of children

Diez perritos [*Ten Little Puppies*] is one of the most popular counting
rhymes in Spanish folklore. It has traveled from Spain to the Americas,
where several versions can be found—each telling the story of how
the ten puppies were lost. We have created our own playful version, in
which the last puppy remains to brighten the life of a child.

Rayo is an imprint of HarperCollins Publishers.

Ten Little Puppies / Diez perritos
Spanish text adaptation copyright © 2011 by Alma Flor Ada and F. Isabel Campoy
English translation copyright © 2011 by Rosalma Zubizaretta
Illustrations copyright © 2011 by Ulises Wensell

All rights reserved. Manufactured in China.
No part of this book may be used or reproduced in any manner whatsoever without written
permission except in the case of brief quotations embodied in critical articles and reviews.
For information address HarperCollins Children's Books, a division of HarperCollins Publishers,
195 Broadway, New York, NY 10007.
www.harpercollinschildrens.com

Library of Congress Cataloging-in-Publication Data is available.
ISBN 978-0-06-147043-1 (trade bdg.) — ISBN 978-0-06-147044-8 (lib. bdg.)

Typography by Jeanne L. Hogle
14 15 SCP 10 9 8 7 6

First Edition

To Victoria Anne, Cristina Isabel, and Jessica Emily—lovers
of puppies—and their siblings and cousins: Timothy, Camille,
Samantha, Daniel, Nicholas, and Collette

To Pablo and Diego IV, who have inherited a beautiful pedigree

—A.F.A. and F.I.C.

To my future grandsons, who will also love dogs

—U.W.

YO TENÍA DIEZ PERRITOS,
DIEZ PERRITOS TENÍA YO…

Yo tenía diez perritos,
yo tenía diez perritos,
uno se fue a ver la nieve
y sólo quedaron nueve,
nueve, nueve, nueve.

OH, I HAD TEN LITTLE PUPPIES,
TEN LITTLE PUPPIES HAD I. . . .

Oh, I had ten little puppies,
Oh, I had ten little puppies,
One went to live where it snows all the time,
So now there are only nine,
Nine, nine, nine, nine, nine.

YO TENÍA NUEVE PERRITOS,
NUEVE PERRITOS TENÍA YO...

De los nueve que quedaban,
de los nueve que quedaban,
uno se comió un bizcocho
y sólo quedaron ocho,
ocho, ocho, ocho.

OH, I HAD NINE LITTLE PUPPIES,
NINE LITTLE PUPPIES HAD I. . . .

Of the nine pups that were left,
Of the nine pups that were left,
One thought pastries tasted great,
So now there are only eight,
Eight, eight, eight, eight, eight.

YO TENÍA OCHO PERRITOS,
OCHO PERRITOS TENÍA YO…

De los ocho que quedaban,
de los ocho que quedaban,
uno fue tras un cohete
y sólo quedaron siete,
siete, siete, siete.

OH, I HAD EIGHT LITTLE PUPPIES,
EIGHT LITTLE PUPPIES HAD I. . . .

Of the eight pups that were left,
Of the eight pups that were left,
One chased after rocket heaven,
So now there are only seven,
Seven, seven, seven.

YO TENÍA SIETE PERRITOS,
SIETE PERRITOS TENÍA YO...

De los siete que quedaban,
de los siete que quedaban,
uno se fue a ver al rey
y sólo quedaron seis,
seis, seis, seis, seis, seis.

OH, I HAD SEVEN LITTLE PUPPIES,
SEVEN LITTLE PUPPIES HAD I. . . .

Of the seven that were left,
Of the seven that were left,
One set out to show the king some tricks,
So now there are only six,
Six, six, six, six, six.

Yo TENÍA SEIS PERRITOS,
SEIS PERRITOS TENÍA YO...

De los seis que me quedaban,
de los seis que me quedaban,
uno se escapó de un brinco
y sólo quedaron cinco,
cinco, cinco, cinco.

OH, I HAD SIX LITTLE PUPPIES,
SIX LITTLE PUPPIES HAD I. . . .

Of the six pups that were left,
Of the six pups that were left,
One ran off with a hop, a skip, and a dive,
So now there are only five,
Five, five, five, five, five.

YO TENÍA CINCO PERRITOS,
CINCO PERRITOS TENÍA YO…

De los cinco que quedaban,
de los cinco que quedaban,
uno se fue tras un gato
y sólo quedaron cuatro,
cuatro, cuatro, cuatro.

OH, I HAD FIVE LITTLE PUPPIES,
FIVE LITTLE PUPPIES HAD I. . . .

Of the five pups that were left,
Of the five pups that were left,
One took off to chase the cat next door,
So now there are only four,
Four, four, four, four, four.

YO TENÍA CUATRO PERRITOS,
CUATRO PERRITOS TENÍA YO…

De los cuatro que quedaban,
de los cuatro que quedaban,
uno se fue con Andrés
y sólo quedaron tres,
tres, tres, tres, tres, tres.

OH, I HAD FOUR LITTLE PUPPIES,
FOUR LITTLE PUPPIES HAD I. . . .

Of the four pups that were left,
of the four pups that were left,
I gave one away to Andres for free,
so now there are only three,
Three, three, three, three, three.

YO TENÍA TRES PERRITOS,
TRES PERRITOS TENÍA YO…

De los tres que me quedaban,
de los tres que me quedaban,
a uno le ha dado la tos
y sólo quedaron dos
dos, dos, dos, dos, dos.

OH, I HAD THREE LITTLE PUPPIES,
THREE LITTLE PUPPIES HAD I. . . .

Of the three pups that were left,
Of the three pups that were left,
One came down with the doggie flu,
So now there are only two,
Two, two, two, two, two.

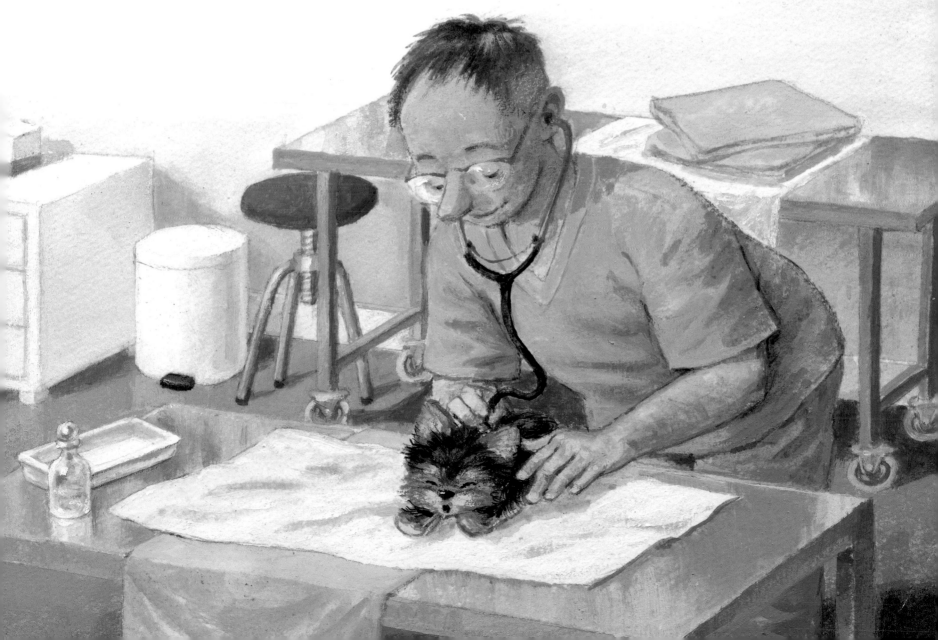

Yo tenía dos perritos,
dos perritos tenía yo…

De los dos que me quedaban,
de los dos que me quedaban,
uno canta con un tuno
y ahora sólo queda uno,
uno, uno, uno.

OH, I HAD TWO LITTLE PUPPIES,
TWO LITTLE PUPPIES HAD I. . . .

Of the two pups that were left,
Of the two pups that were left,
One wanted to sing with Juan,
So now there is only one,
One, one, one, one, one.

AHORA YO TENGO UN PERRITO,
UN PERRITO TENGO YO…

Y el último que quedaba
y el último que quedaba
permanecerá a mi lado:
¡Es mi perrito adorado!
¡Muy, muy bien amado!

OH, NOW I HAVE JUST ONE PUPPY,
JUST ONE PUPPY HAVE I. . . .

And the one pup I have now,
And the one pup I have now,
He will never, ever go,
'Cause he knows I love him so,
Love, love, love him so.

Diez perritos
Ten Little Puppies

Yo te - ní - a diez pe - rri - tos, yo te -
Oh, I had ten lit - tle pup - pies, Oh, I

ní - a diez pe - rri - tos, u - no se fue a ver la____ nie - ve,____ y só -
had ten lit - tle pup - pies, One__ went to__ live where it snows all the time, so__

lo que__ - da - ron nue - ve, nue - ve, nue - ve, nue - ve.
now there are on - ly nine,__ Nine, nine, nine, nine, nine.__

Diez perritos

Yo tenía diez perritos,
yo tenía diez perritos,
uno se fue a ver la nieve
y sólo quedaron nueve,
nueve, nueve, nueve.

De los nueve que quedaban,
de los nueve que quedaban,
uno se comió un bizcocho
y sólo quedaron ocho,
ocho, ocho, ocho.

De los ocho que quedaban,
de los ocho que quedaban,
uno fue tras un cohete
y sólo quedaron siete,
siete, siete, siete.

De los siete que quedaban,
de los siete que quedaban,
uno se fue a ver al rey
y sólo quedaron seis,
seis, seis, seis, seis, seis.

De los seis que me quedaban,
de los seis que me quedaban,
uno se escapó de un brinco
y sólo quedaron cinco,
cinco, cinco, cinco.

De los cinco que quedaban,
de los cinco que quedaban,
uno se fue tras un gato
y sólo quedaron cuatro,
cuatro, cuatro, cuatro.

De los cuatro que quedaban,
de los cuatro que quedaban,
uno se fue con Andrés
y sólo quedaron tres,
tres, tres, tres, tres, tres.

De los tres que me quedaban,
de los tres que me quedaban,
a uno le ha dado la tos
y sólo quedaron dos
dos, dos, dos, dos, dos.

De los dos que me quedaban,
de los dos que me quedaban,
uno canta con un tuno
y ahora sólo queda uno,
uno, uno, uno.

Y el último que quedaba
y el último que quedaba
permanecerá a mi lado:
¡Es mi perrito adorado!
¡Muy, muy bien amado!

Ten Little Puppies

Oh, I had ten little puppies,
Oh, I had ten little puppies,
One went to live where it snows
    all the time,
So now there are only nine,
Nine, nine, nine, nine, nine.

Of the nine pups that were left,
Of the nine pups that were left,
One thought pastries tasted great,
So now there are only eight,
Eight, eight, eight, eight, eight.

Of the eight pups that were left,
Of the eight pups that were left,
One chased after rocket heaven,
So now there are only seven,
Seven, seven, seven.

Of the seven that were left,
Of the seven that were left,
One set out to show the king some
    tricks,
So now there are only six,
Six, six, six, six, six.

Of the six pups that were left,
Of the six pups that were left,
One ran off with a hop, a skip, and
    a dive,
So now there are only five,
Five, five, five, five, five.

Of the five pups that were left,
Of the five pups that were left,
One took off to chase the cat next
    door,
So now there are only four,
Four, four, four, four, four.

Of the four pups that were left,
Of the four pups that were left,
I gave one away to Andres for free,
So now there are only three,
Three, three, three, three, three.

Of the three pups that were left,
Of the three pups that were left,
One came down with the doggie
    flu,
So now there are only two,
Two, two, two, two, two.

Of the two pups that were left,
Of the two pups that were left,
One wanted to sing with Juan,
So now there is only one,
One, one, one, one, one.

And the one pup I have now,
And the one pup I have now,
He will never, ever go,
'Cause he knows I love him so,
Love, love, love him so.

Siberian Husky / Husky siberiano

In cold Arctic regions, huskies work hard pulling sleds and herding reindeer. They are playful, loving, and so friendly that they do not make good guard dogs.

En las frías regiones árticas, los perros husky sibereanos tiran de los trineos y ayudan a pastorear a los renos. Son juguetones, amantes de su familia y tan amistosos que no son buenos perros guardianes.

Basset Hound / Basset hound

In addition to a great sense of smell, these hound dogs have very short legs, long bodies, and velvety ears. Loyal and affectionate, they make wonderful pets. When they want attention, their low murmuring whine almost sounds like "talking"!

Estos perros de caza, con gran sentido del olfato, tienen patas muy cortas, cuerpos alargados y orejas aterciopeladas. Son excelentes mascotas, fieles y afectuosos. Para llamar la atención murmuran y parecería que hablaran.

Fox Terrier / Fox terrier

If you are not afraid of being outsmarted by your dog or of having her run circles around you, then you are ready to own a fox terrier. With short-haired tricolor coats, these intelligent dogs are agile and quickly learn tricks.

Si no tienes miedo de que tu perro se salga con la suya o de que resulte más listo que tú, entonces puedes tener un fox terrier. Estos perros inteligentes de corto pelaje tricolor son ágiles y capaces de hacer trucos.

Collie / Pastor escocés o *collie*

Have you seen any of Lassie's films? If so, you know that collies are noble and very protective of their loved ones. They have served as sheepdogs for centuries and can also learn to do search and rescue.

¿Has visto alguna de las películas de Lassie? Entonces ya sabes que los *collies* son nobles y protectores de sus seres queridos. Han sido perros pastores por siglos. También sirven para la búsqueda y el rescate.

Dalmatian / Dálmata

A long time ago in the United States, when fire trucks used to be pulled by horses, Dalmatians would run ahead to clear the way. They also helped firefighters rescue people from fires. That's why they are still known as "firehouse dogs."

En los Estados Unidos, cuando los carros de bomberos eran tirados por caballos, los dálmatas corrían por delante para abrirles paso. También ayudaban a rescatar víctimas en los incendios. Por eso se convirtieron en mascota de los bomberos.

Saint Bernard / San Bernardo

Saint Bernards are huge, calm, and dignified and have all the makings of a true and loyal friend. They can find someone who has been buried under many feet of snow and keep that person warm until other rescuers arrive.

Los perros San Bernardo son enormes, calmados y dignos. La verdadera definición de "amigo". Pueden encontrar a una persona sepultada bajo muchos pies de nieve y calentarla hasta que lleguen otros a rescatarla.

Poodle / Caniche

Whether full size, toy, or miniature, these curly-haired dogs are elegant and good-natured runners, perfect friends for any occasion.

Ya sean grandes, medianos o miniatura, estos perros de pelo rizado son elegantes, de buena naturaleza y buenos corredores. Son amigos perfectos en toda ocasión.

Yorkshire Terrier / Yorkshire terrier

These small, feisty dogs with long silky coats love to bark. Brave, clever, and strong-willed, they can be the hero of any battle.

A estos perros diminutos de largo pelo sedoso les encanta ladrar. Bravos y astutos, con una personalidad decidida podrían ser los héroes de cualquier batalla.

Cocker Spaniel /Cocker spaniel

All you need to see is their wagging tails to know that cocker spaniels are friendly and playful dogs. As lovely as they look with their glamorous silken coats all cleaned and brushed, they still love to roll around in the woods and come home covered with burrs and twigs!

Sólo hay que verlos agitar la cola para saber que los perros cocker spaniel son juguetones y amistosos. A pesar de verse glamorosos envueltos en su abrigo sedoso bien cepillado, les encanta corretear en los bosques y regresar a casa cubiertos de cáscaras y ramitas.

Samoyed / Samoyedo

Friendly and playful, these white Arctic dogs were among the first to be domesticated by human beings. The nomadic Nenets bred the Samoyed for herding reindeer and pulling sleds, and slept next to their dogs at night to stay warm during the cold Arctic winters.

Estos hermosos perros blancos del Ártico, juguetones y amistosos, han sido de los primeros perros domesticados por los seres humanos. Los miembros de la tribu nómada nenet los usaban para tirar de sus trineos y pastorear a los renos, y dormían con ellos para calentarse durante las frías noches árticas.

APR 0 3 2016